For my cruising buddies:
Josh, Joey, Bobby, and Frankie—K. D.

For JK, *beep-beep vroom*—M. P.

BEACH LANE BOOKS

An imprint of Simon & Schuster Children's Publishing Division
1230 Avenue of the Americas, New York, New York 10020
Text copyright © 2018 by Kate Dopirak
Illustrations copyright © 2018 by Mary Peterson
All rights reserved, including the right of reproduction in whole or in part in any form.
BEACH LANE BOOKS is a trademark of Simon & Schuster, Inc.
For information about special discounts for bulk purchases, please contact Simon & Schuster Special Sales
at1-866-506-1949 or business@simonandschuster.com.
The Simon & Schuster Speakers Bureau can bring authors to your live event. For more information or to book an event,
contact the Simon & Schuster Speakers Bureau at 1-866-248-3049 or visit our website at www.simonspeakers.com.
Book design by Lauren Rille
The text for this book was set in Futura.
The illustrations for this book were rendered in hand-printed linoleum blocks, then digitally collaged.
Manufactured in China
1117 SCP
First Edition
10 9 8 7 6 5 4 3 2 1
CIP data for this book is available from the Library of Congress.
ISBN 978-1-4814-8803-7 (hardcover)
ISBN 978-1-4814-8804-4 (eBook)

Twinkle, Twinkle, Little Car

written by Kate Dopirak   illustrated by Mary Peterson

Beach Lane Books ★ New York London Toronto Sydney New Delhi

Twinkle, twinkle, little car,
how you love to travel far!

Now it's time to go to bed.
But you want to drive instead.

Hit your headlights. Hang a right.
Cruise around to say good night.

Honk to tractors in their shed.
They're already tucked in bed.

Beep!
Beep!

Airplane swoops across the sky.
Vroom-vroom-zooms as you pass by.

Open windows. Drop the top.
Race to town before you stop.

Trucks and taxis, buses too—

they all toot good night to you.

Swish your wipers. Blink your lights.
Set the station in your sights.

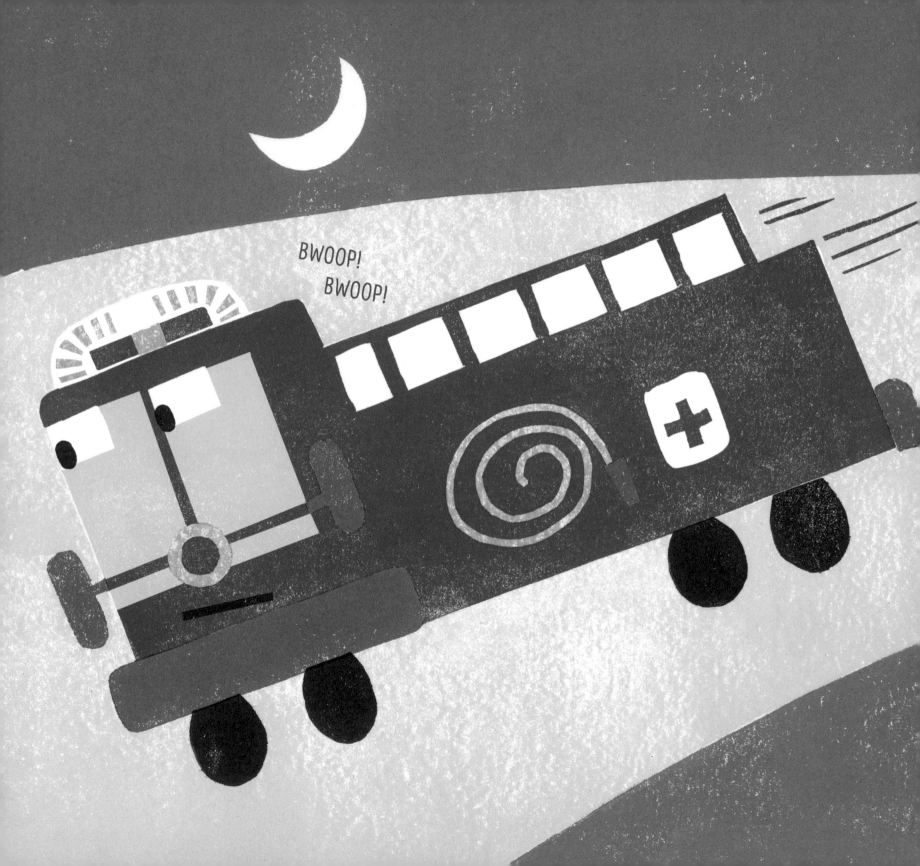

BEE-BOOO!

BEE-BOOO!

Sirens whoop and whistles blow.
What a flashy good-night show!

Roll through the construction site.
Cranes and diggers wave good night.

Take a pit stop in the park.
Now it's getting really dark.

See the ferry. Motor on.
Muffle back a vroomy yawn.

Uh-oh, tank is running low.
Engine purrs, then starts to slow.

Putt-putt home and pull right in . . .

and let your beep-beep dreams begin.